CAMILA
THE VIDEO STAR

written by *ALICIA SALAZAR*

illustrated by *THAIS DAMIÃO*

PICTU

Camila the Star is published by Picture Window Books,
an imprint of Capstone.
1710 Roe Crest Drive
North Mankato, Minnesota 56003
www.capstonepub.com

Library of Congress Cataloging-in-Publication Data
Names: Salazar, Alicia, 1973– author. | Damião, Thais, illustrator.
Title: Camila the video star / by Alicia Salazar; illustrated by Thais Damião.
Description: North Mankato, Minnesota : Picture Window Books, a Capstone
imprint, [2021] | Series: Camila the star | Includes glossary, glossary of Spanish
words, activities, and discussion questions. | Audience: Ages 5–7. | Audience:
Grades K–1. | Summary: "A video contest is the perfect way for Camila to
become a star. To enter, she must make a video that explains what her city, Los
Angeles, means to her. But Los Angeles is so big-how will she decide what to
talk about? As Camila works on her video, she realizes that there's one special
thing that makes her city feel like home"— Provided by publisher.
Identifiers: LCCN 2020025196 (print) | LCCN 2020025197 (ebook) | ISBN
9781515882114 (library binding) | ISBN 9781515883203 (paperback) | ISBN
9781515891840 (pdf)
Subjects: CYAC: Video recordings—Production and direction—Fiction. |
Contests—Fiction. | Neighborhoods—Fiction. | Los Angeles (Calif.)—Fiction. |
Hispanic Americans—Fiction.
Classification: LCC PZ7.1.S2483 Cd 2021 (print) | LCC PZ7.1.S2483 (ebook) |
DDC [E]—dc23
LC record available at https://lccn.loc.gov/2020025196
LC ebook record available at https://lccn.loc.gov/2020025197

Designer: Kay Fraser

TABLE OF CONTENTS

Meet Camila and Her Family

Papá

Mamá

Ana, age 14

Andres, age 10

Camila, age 7

Spanish Glossary

amigo (ah-MEE-goh)—friend

buenas tardes (BWEH-nahs TAHR-dehs)—good afternoon

buenos días (BWEH-nohs DEE-ahs)—good morning

hola (OH-lah)—hello

Mamá (mah-MAH)—Mom

maraca (muh-RAH-kuh)—a musical instruments similar to a rattle

Papá (pah-PAH)—Dad

señor (seh-NYOR)—man or mister

señora (seh-NYOH-rah)—woman or madam

Chapter 1

THE CONTEST

Camila was excited about a new contest. "I will be a star!" she said.

It was a video contest. Contestants had to make a video saying what makes Los Angeles special to them.

The winning video would be shown on the TV show *Hola, Los Angeles*. The winner would be a guest on the show.

"I just have to win that contest," said Camila. "Then I will be a TV star!"

The contest had three rules.

HOLA, LOS ANGELES

CITY-WIDE VIDEO CONTEST

1. The video must be three minutes
2. No help from professionals allowed
3. Must have permission from a parent

Camila explained the video contest to Mamá.

"That sounds like a great contest!" said Mamá. "What makes Los Angeles special to you, Camila?"

"I made a list!" said Camila, waving her paper. "Now I can work on my video!"

≡SPECIAL≡
LOS ANGELES

1. The Hollywood sign
2. The Santa Monica Pier
3. The Walk of Fame

Chapter 2

SPECIAL PLACES

Camila wrote a video script, "The Hollywood sign is one of the most famous places in the world . . ."

Her sister, Ana, looked over her shoulder. "Do you even remember going to the Hollywood sign?" asked Ana. "You were three."

"But everyone thinks the Hollywood sign is special," said Camila.

"But do *you*?" asked Ana. "What makes Los Angeles special to you?"

Camila considered Ana's question. She couldn't think of anything that wasn't famous.

She thought about it when she went to the farmers' market with her parents.

"**Buenos dias**," said Señor Reyes. He gave them each a milk candy. "A treat for **amigos**!"

She thought about it
when her family went to the
neighborhood bakery.

"**Buenas tardes**," Señora
Ortiz said. She pinched Camila's
cheek. Then she gave Camila
tongs to pick out her favorite
Mexican sweet bread.

Camila thought about it when
she went to the flea market. Her
neighbor Señora Martinez had a
stand full of toys and games.

"**Hola**, Camila," she said.
"You might need some **maracas**
for a dance routine." She stuffed
a pair of maracas into Camila's
backpack.

Camila looked at Señora Martinez. She loved her soft smile and her sing-song voice.

Camila knew what she wanted to write about.

Chapter 3

THE VIDEO

With her brother's help, Camila made her video. It was about all of the special people who lived in her neighborhood.

She talked about their kindness and warmth. She talked about how generous they were.

She talked about how they
made her neighborhood a
wonderful place to call home.

Camila uploaded the video onto the show's website to enter the contest.

She tapped her foot and paced for two weeks. She watched the other video entries. They were mostly about famous places.

Finally, she heard the news. "The winner of the video contest is . . . Camila Maria Flores Ortiz!"

Camila couldn't believe it. She was so excited, she jumped up and down for a whole minute!

Now everyone would know about her special neighborhood.

The next week, Camila visited the set of *Hola, Los Angeles*. It was time for her interview.

"Your video won the city video contest. How do you feel?" asked the host.

Camila stared at the camera with wide eyes.

"I feel like a star!" she said.

Make a Video About Your Neighborhood

Camila's video celebrated and honored her neighborhood and the people who live there. Make a video to celebrate your neighborhood. If you don't have a device to record with, no problem! You can share your thoughts with a speech or essay.

WHAT YOU NEED
- paper
- something to write with
- a device such as a smartphone or tablet

WHAT YOU DO

1. Brainstorm three things you love about your neighborhood. Write them down.

2. Now write your script. It should explain what makes each thing important to you. Use your script to convince others that your neighborhood is a special place. Revise your script until you have it just right.

3. When your script is ready, it is time to record. For a simple video, you can record yourself reading your script as you share photos or drawings of the things you are talking about. For a fancier video, use video software that lets you record videos or images and add a voice recording. (Ask an adult for help if you need it!)

4. Share your video with your friends and family!

Glossary

consider (kuhn-SID-er)—to think about

contestant (kuhn-TES-tuhnt)—a person who takes part in a contest

farmers' market (FAR-mers MAR-kit)—a shopping area where people sell the items they grow and make

generous (JEN-er-uhs)—willing to share

interview (IN-ter-vyoo)—a meeting where a person asks questions to find out more about something

neighborhood (NAY-bur-hood)—a small area in a town or city where people live

pace (PAYSS)—to walk with slow, steady steps as a way to deal with nervous feelings

routine (roo-TEEN)—a set of dance steps that are carefully worked out for practice and performance

script (SKRIPT)—a written plan for a video

Think About the Story

1. What steps did Camila take to enter the video contest? Write them out.

2. Camila listed famous places in Los Angeles. Then she thought about special places in her own neighborhood. Are there any famous places where you live? What places in your neighborhood are special to you? Make two lists.

3. How do you think Camila felt after she entered the contest but before she heard the result? What are some clues from the story that tell us how she's feeling?

4. We learn about some of Camila's special neighbors in this story. Write a paragraph about a special neighbor you have.

About the Author

Alicia Salazar is a Mexican American children's book author who has written for blogs, magazines, and educational publishers. She was also once an elementary school teacher and a marine biologist. She currently lives in the suburbs of Houston, Texas, but is a city girl at heart. When Alicia is not dreaming up new adventures to experience, she is turning her adventures into stories for kids.

About the Illustrator

Thais Damião is a Brazilian illustrator and graphic designer. Born and raised in a small city in Rio de Janeiro, Brazil, she spent her childhood playing with her brother and cousins and drawing all the time. Her illustrations are dedicated to children and inspired by nature and friendship. Thais currently lives in California.